PHOENIX

APEX

BY CHRISTINE HA

WWW.APEXEDITIONS.COM

Apex is distributed by North Star Editions:
sales@northstareditions.com | 888-417-0195

Produced for Apex by Red Line Editorial.

Photographs ©: Shutterstock Images, cover, 1, 4–5, 6–7, 8, 10–11, 15, 16–17, 20–21, 22–23, 24, 25, 26–27, 29; iStockphoto, 9, 12–13, 14; Charles Walker Collection/Alamy, 18–19

Library of Congress Control Number: 2020952926

ISBN
978-1-63738-023-9 (hardcover)
978-1-63738-059-8 (paperback)
978-1-63738-128-1 (ebook pdf)
978-1-63738-095-6 (hosted ebook)

Printed in the United States of America
Mankato, MN
082021

NOTE TO PARENTS AND EDUCATORS

Apex books are designed to build literacy skills in striving readers. Exciting, high-interest content attracts and holds readers' attention. The text is carefully leveled to allow students to achieve success quickly. Additional features, such as bolded glossary words for difficult terms, help build comprehension.

TABLE OF CONTENTS

CHAPTER 1

FROM THE ASHES

The sun is rising. The phoenix soars across the sky. Its feathers shine with bright colors.

The phoenix appears in some stories about the worship of the sun.

The phoenix lands in its nest. Then it bursts into flames. Branches crackle and snap as the fire grows.

In some stories, the phoenix makes its nest in a palm tree. In others, it flies to a temple for the god of the sun.

One story says the phoenix shoots out rays of sunshine.

Finally, the fire dies down. Only a pile of ash is left. But the phoenix is not dead. Instead, it is reborn. A new bird rises from the ashes.

The phoenix's eyes and feathers can glow like fire.

The phoenix is said to be invincible. This means it cannot be hurt.

A BEAUTIFUL SONG

When the phoenix is about to die, it builds a nest from wood and spices. Then the bird sits down. It begins to sing. The song is very beautiful. After the song ends, the nest catches fire.

RESVRGAM

CHAPTER 2

FIERY BIRD

Stories of the phoenix began in **ancient** times. The **legends** tell of a magical bird that can live forever.

A phoenix decorates St. Paul's Cathedral in London, England.

Like a peacock, a phoenix can have a long tail.

The bird has beautiful feathers. They are often red, orange, and gold. They can be purple, too. Some stories say the bird looks like an eagle. Others say it is like a peacock.

Some stories say the phoenix's eyes are like blue gems.

There is only one phoenix. But every 500 years, it sets itself on fire to be born again.

The phoenix appears in art from around the world. It's often a symbol of rebirth.

Each time the phoenix burns, it becomes young again.

The phoenix appears on some countries' coins.

HEALING TEARS

As legends spread, people add new details. In some stories, the phoenix can change sizes. In others, its tears have the power to heal people.

CHAPTER 3

ANCIENT ORIGINS

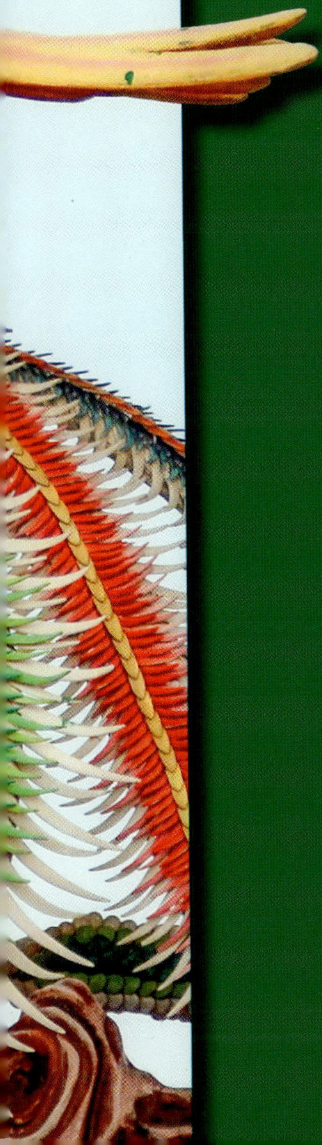

The phoenix appears in Greek **myths**. But those stories are based on earlier tales from Egypt.

Stories of legendary birds come from around the world.

The Egyptians told stories of a bird called the Bennu. Like the sun, it rose each morning to be reborn.

The Bennu bird appears in the Book of the Dead. This book was written in ancient Egypt.

Stories said the Bennu helped create the world. The bird had close ties to the Egyptian sun god, Ra.

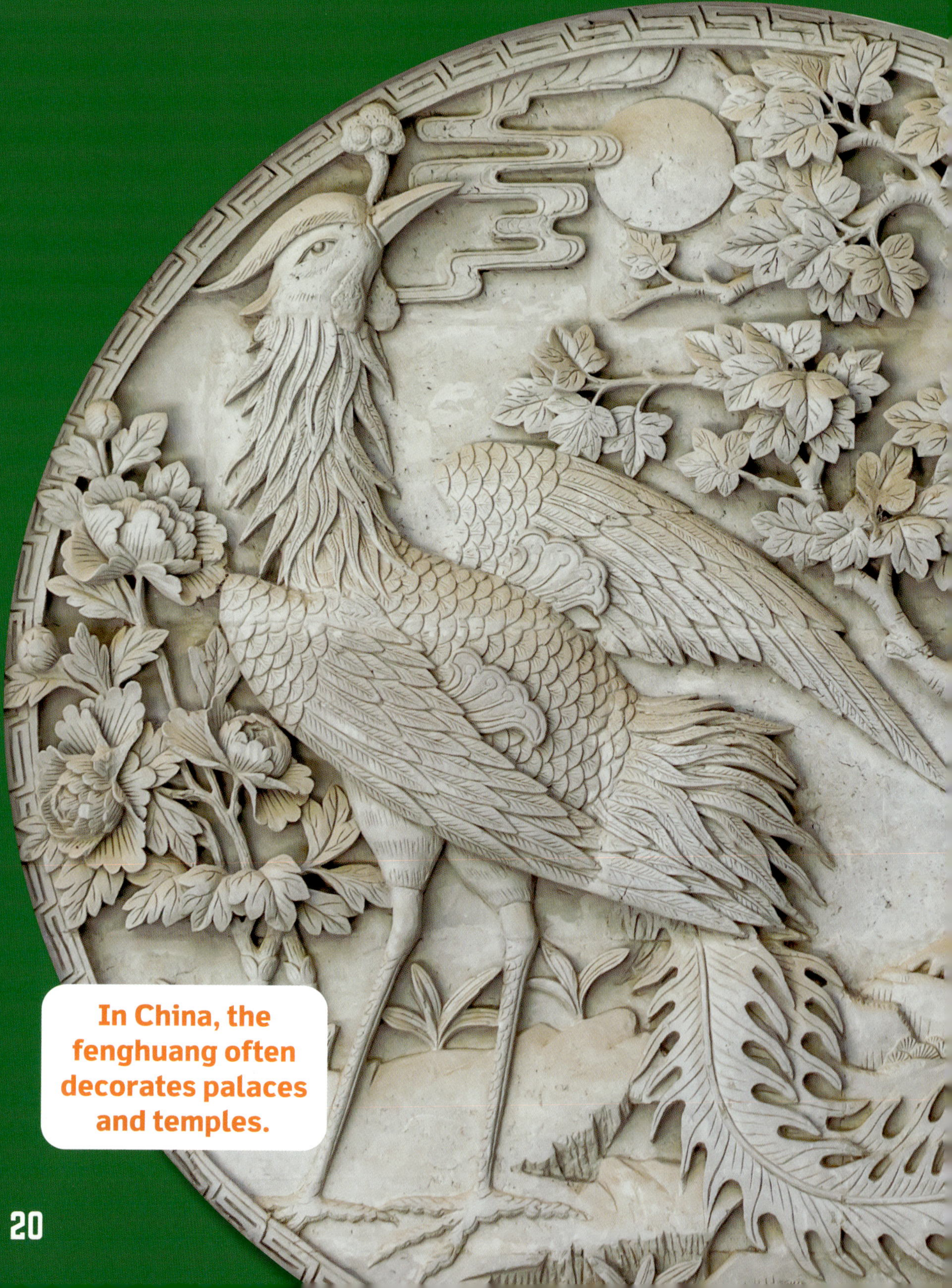

In China, the fenghuang often decorates palaces and temples.

Later, a Greek **historian** wrote these stories down. The stories spread around the world. Other **cultures** have similar legends. Many are about hope and rebirth.

SIMILAR STORIES

Chinese legends tell of the fenghuang. Like a phoenix, this bird is **immortal**. People rarely see it. But when they do, it's a sign of peace and good luck.

CHAPTER 4

BIRD BONES

People often create myths to explain things they don't fully understand. What happens after death is a common topic.

The phoenix is a symbol in several religions.

Legends may also be based on **fossils**. People find the bones of ancient animals. They guess what those animals looked like.

Fossils can give people a general sense of what animals looked like.

Stories of the firebird inspired a famous ballet.

Russian folktales tell of the firebird. It has magical feathers.

The Goliath heron is the largest heron alive today. It's almost 5 feet (1.5 m) tall.

Long ago, a huge kind of heron lived in Egypt. People may have found this bird's bones. They may have told legends about the phoenix to explain the bones.

A HUGE HERON

In modern times, scientists studied the huge heron's bones. They named it the Bennu heron. They think it grew more than 6.5 feet (2 m) tall.

COMPREHENSION QUESTIONS

Write your answers on a separate piece of paper.

1. Write two sentences explaining the key ideas of Chapter 3.

2. Would you want to live forever like a phoenix? Why or why not?

3. What large bird's fossils may have been the basis for legends of the phoenix?

   A. eagle
   B. heron
   C. peacock

4. How could writing a legend down help it spread?

   A. People had no way to spread the legend before.
   B. People could change what the legend said.
   C. People in other times and places could learn about the legend.

5. What does **ash** mean in this book?

Finally, the fire dies down. Only a pile of ***ash*** *is left.*

A. a type of food
B. leaves on a tree
C. small bits of burned wood

6. What does **rarely** mean in this book?

People ***rarely*** *see it. But when they do, it's a sign of peace and good luck.*

A. not very often
B. all the time
C. never

Answer key on page 32.

GLOSSARY

ancient

Very old or from long ago.

cultures

Groups of people and the ways they live, including their beliefs and laws.

folktales

Stories that have been told out loud for many years.

fossils

Remains of plants and animals that lived long ago.

historian

A person who studies and writes about the past.

immortal

Able to live forever.

legends

Famous stories about people, creatures, or events, often based on facts but sometimes not completely true.

myths

Well-known stories from the past that often include magic.

symbol

An object or idea that stands for and reminds people of something else.

TO LEARN MORE

BOOKS

Gagne, Tammy. *Egyptian Gods, Heroes, and Mythology.* Minneapolis: Abdo Publishing, 2019.

Sautter, A. J. *Discover Dragons, Giants, and Other Deadly Fantasy Monsters*. Mankato, MN: Capstone Press, 2018.

Troupe, Thomas Kingsley. *Phoenixes*. Minneapolis, Bellwether Media, 2021.

ONLINE RESOURCES

Visit **www.apexeditions.com** to find links and resources related to this title.

ABOUT THE AUTHOR

Christine Ha lives in Minnesota. She enjoys reading mythology and urban legends from around the world.

INDEX

Answer Key:
1. Answers will vary; **2.** Answers will vary; **3.** B; **4.** C; **5.** C; **6.** A